WIN A NAUGHTY FAIRIES T-SHIRT!

Every time those Naughty Fairies
are hatching a plan they do their fairy code
where they come up with NF words...

Niggle Flaptart
Nicely Framed
Nimble Fingers

Can you help the Naughty Fairies
find two more words beginning with
N.................. and F..................?

Each month we will select the best entries to win a very special Naughty Fairies T-shirt and they will go into the draw to have their NF idea printed in the next lot of books!

Don't forget to include your name and address.
Send your entry to: Naughty Fairies NF Competition,
Hodder Children's Marketing, 338 Euston Road,
London NW1 3BH.
Australian readers should write to:
Hachette Children's Books, Level 17/207 Kent Street,
Sydney, NSW 2000

For ... o.uk/terms

Collect all the Naughty Fairies books:

1. Imps are Wimps
2. Wand in the Pond
3. Caterpillar Thriller
4. Sweet Cheat
5. Bumble Rumble
6. Spells and Smells
7. Tricksy Pixie
8. An Utter Flutter
9. Never Hug a Slug
10. Potion Commotion
11. Ping's Wings
12. Spider Insider

Ping's Wings

Lucy Mayflower

A [illegible] of Hachette Children's Books

Special thanks to Lucy Courtenay

Created by Hodder Children's Books and Lucy Courtenay

Illustrations created by Artful Doodlers

First published in Great Britain in 2007
by Hodder Children's Books

1

A Catalogue record for this book is available from the British Library

IISBN – 10: 0 340 94432 3
ISBN – 13: 978 0 340 94432 5

Printed and bound in Great Britain
by Bookmarque Ltd, Croydon, Surrey

The paper and board used in this paperback by Hodder Children's Books are natural recyclable products made from wood grown in sustainable forests. The manufacturing processes conform to the environmental regulations of the country of origin.

Hodder Children's Books
A division of Hachette Children's Books
338 Euston Rd, London NW1 3BH

Contents

Ambrosia Academy
WOOD STUMP

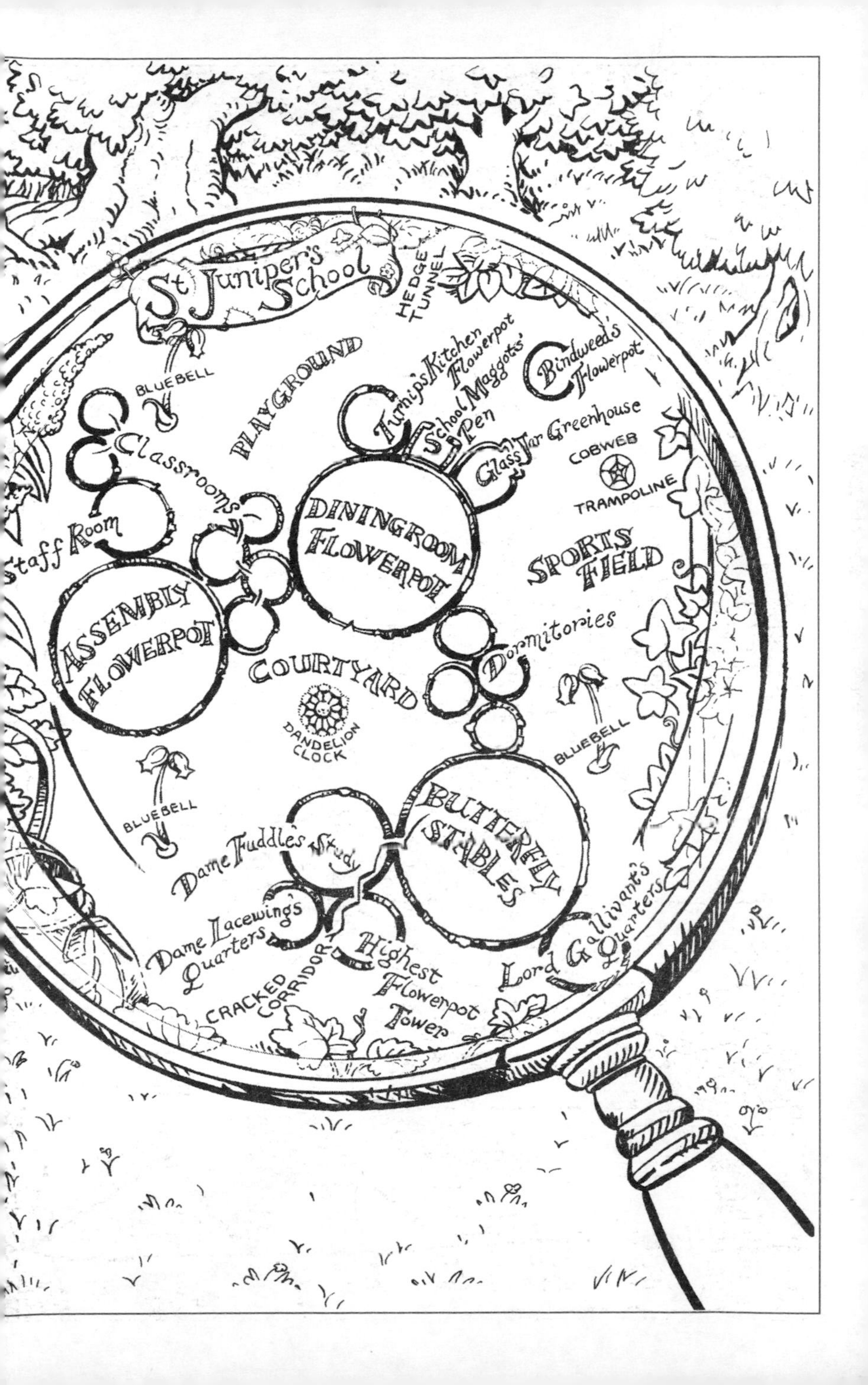
St Juniper's School
HEDGE TUNNEL
PLAYGROUND
BLUEBELL
Classrooms
Staff Room
Turnip's Kitchen Flowerpot
School Maggots' Pen
Bindweed's Flowerpot
Glass Jar Greenhouse
COBWEB TRAMPOLINE
DININGROOM FLOWERPOT
SPORTS FIELD
ASSEMBLY FLOWERPOT
COURTYARD
DANDELION CLOCK
Dormitories
BLUEBELL
BLUEBELL
BUTTERFLY STABLES
Dame Fuddles' Study
Dame Lacewing's Quarters
CRACKED CORRIDOR
Highest Flowerpot Tower
Lord Gallivant's Quarters

1

The New Committee

Down at the bottom of the garden, a worried conversation could be heard inside one of the flowerpot towers of St Juniper's School for Fairies.

"What do you mean, *all six fairies* on the Bluebell Ball Committee are on detention tonight?" asked Dame Fuddle, Head of St Juniper's. "What about tonight's Bluebell Ball Committee Meeting? There must be some mistake, Lavender!"

"There's no mistake, Fenella," said the tall, thin-faced fairy beside the door in a weary voice.

"But the Bluebell Ball is in *four days' time*!" said Dame Fuddle, her exclamation marks sounding louder than usual. "There will be so much to do at this final meeting! Whatever have our committee fairies done?"

"Two of them broke into Next-Door's Garden to steal rose petals for balldresses," said Dame Lacewing. "Two more made a potion to turn their hair blonde."

"Did it work?" asked Dame Fuddle.

"It blew up, broke three window panes and turned one of them into a fieldmouse," said Dame Lacewing.

Dame Fuddle looked anxious. "What about the other two?"

"One unwound all the spider silk from the cobweb trampoline to weave into a silver ball cloak," said Dame Lacewing. "And one has refused to eat anything this week in order to fit into her dress."

"Surely that doesn't deserve a detention?" asked Dame Fuddle.

"Because she hadn't eaten anything,

she fell asleep in my Maths lesson," said Dame Lacewing. "This Bluebell Ball is more trouble than it's worth."

"How can you say such a thing, Lavender!" Dame Fuddle gasped, fanning herself with a large petal. "The Bluebell Ball only takes place at the May blue moon, which only happens – well, once in a blue moon! It is the most important social event in the fairy calendar! Even *you* must be looking forward to it!"

"Must I," said Dame Lacewing grimly. She took a sip of chicory coffee from her cup.

"Of course you must!" said Dame Fuddle, ignoring Dame Lacewing's tone of voice and helping herself to a sugared buttercup. "The Bluebell Feast! The gowns, the royalty, the dancing!" The Head of St Juniper's looked misty-eyed. "I remember my first Bluebell Ball! I danced with the most marvellous

elf . . ." Her voice trailed away and her cheeks turned pink.

"Without a committee," said Dame Lacewing, "we can't attend tonight's final meeting. Important decisions will be made without us."

"We must form an emergency committee!" Dame Fuddle declared. She put down her sugared buttercup in great excitement. "What about Brilliance and her friends? There are six of them, I believe? And of ball age too! Brilliance is such a pretty little thing! She'd represent St Juniper's marvellously!"

Dame Lacewing spilt her cup of chicory coffee. "*Brilliance?*" she repeated. "Brilliance is the naughtiest fairy in the school! Her friend Nettle isn't much better. Tiptoe and Sesame – well, they spend their time giggling, eating or playing with insects. I wouldn't trust Ping within a thousand millisquirts of a committee meeting,

and as for Kelpie and that smelly bumblebee of hers . . ." Dame Lacewing ran out of words.

"High spirits!" said Dame Fuddle fondly. "That's what this Ball Committee needs! They shall join us tonight, Lavender! Ah, what fun we shall all have!"

Out in the school courtyard, the Naughty Fairies were playing with a shiny brown flea they had found in the Nettle Patch that afternoon.

"If you tickle him here, then he jumps like crazy," said Sesame, a small fairy with a fat plait down her back. "Watch."

"Whoa!" A grubby blonde fairy wearing a pair of spider earrings fell back on her bottom as the flea soared into the air and landed on top of the highest flowerpot tower.

"Good job you've got a big bum, Nettle," said the prettiest fairy with a

toss of her wild black hair.

"Speak for yourself, Brilliance," said Nettle, rubbing her bottom.

"I'm going to call him Boing," said Sesame fondly.

The flea scratched himself and stared down at the fairies with shiny black eyes.

"Make him do it again, Sesame," said the smallest fairy eagerly.

Sesame made a chirruping noise. "Boing, Boing, Boing!" she called.

The flea waggled his back legs and jumped back down into the courtyard.

"You're not watching the flea, Kelpie," said the smallest fairy, glancing across at a red-haired fairy with a hairy bumblebee in her lap. "He's fantastic."

Kelpie glanced up. "I *am* watching Flea," she objected, stroking her bumblebee. "I'm watching him very closely, Tiptoe. I think he's got a bit of a temperature."

Flea the bumblebee coughed.

"Not *that* Flea, silly" said Tiptoe. "*This* flea."

"I could train Boing to jump in through a classroom window," suggested the spiky-haired fairy sitting underneath the dandelion clock in the middle of the courtyard. "Maybe in the middle of Fairy Science. They train fleas in China."

"You've never been to China, Ping," said Brilliance.

"So?" challenged Ping. "I still bet I could train him."

Getting tired of standing still, Boing the flea jumped again. This time, he soared right over the flowerpots and disappeared into the Nettle Patch.

"Oh!" Sesame said in disappointment. "He's gone!"

"Let's go and catch him again," suggested Tiptoe.

The Naughty Fairies headed for the Nettle Patch. As they passed Dame

Fuddle's study, the flowerpot door opened. Dame Lacewing stepped out slowly, with her pet beetle Pipsqueak trotting at her ankles.

The Naughty Fairies gave Dame Lacewing their best and most innocent smiles. Dame Lacewing looked at them with suspicion.

"Evening, Dame Lacewing," offered Brilliance.

"Dame Fuddle wishes to see you all in her office," said the Deputy Head with a funny expression on her face.

"I'm sure I heard Dame Lacewing just say *Nature help us all*," said Sesame, peering over her shoulder as the Deputy Head disappeared into her own flowerpot and shut the door.

"It was just your imagination," said Brilliance.

"I wonder why Dame Fuddle wants to see us?" asked Ping.

"We haven't done anything naughty

lately," said Nettle, frowning. "At least, nothing *that* naughty."

"Only one way to find out," said Kelpie, draping Flea around her neck like an enormous woolly scarf.

And cautiously, the Naughty Fairies pushed open Dame Fuddle's study door.

2
The Meeting

"You're speechless, I know!" said Dame Fuddle, as the Naughty Fairies stood before her desk and gawped at her. "Representing St Juniper's on the Bluebell Ball Committee is every young fairy's dream!"

"More like a nightmare," muttered Kelpie.

"Why us, Dame Fuddle?" Ping asked.

"The usual committee is . . . busy tonight!" said Dame Fuddle brightly. Her exclamation marks grew more vigorous. "You'll take part in some very important decisions! It's an immense honour! Sugared buttercup, anyone?"

The Naughty Fairies helped

themselves to sugared buttercups. Tiptoe had two.

"Do we have to decide right now?" asked Brilliance.

"The decision's already made!" said Dame Fuddle, suddenly sounding brisk. "Now off you go, and . . ." She looked doubtfully at Kelpie's dirty black and yellow bumblewool dress and Nettle's

muddy trousers. "Try to . . . tidy yourselves up a bit! We must leave in exactly ten dandelion seeds' time!"

The Naughty Fairies trailed outside.

"I'd rather have a detention than go to the Bluebell Ball Committee Meeting," said Nettle.

"I really wanted to find Boing again," sighed Sesame.

"Maybe there will be food," said Tiptoe hopefully.

A dandelion seed fell off the dandelion clock in the courtyard.

"Nine dandelion seeds of freedom left," said Nettle in a doomed voice.

"Let's go and get changed," said Brilliance.

Kelpie looked down at her black and yellow bumblewool dress. "Into what?" she said. "I've only got this."

"I'll lend you a dress," said Ping. "You're a bit taller than me, but I'm sure I can find something."

"It better not be frilly," warned Kelpie. "And I'm bringing Flea, whether Dame Fuddle likes it or not. He's too sick to leave on his own."

Eight dandelion seeds later, the Naughty Fairies had gathered in the courtyard again. Nettle had washed her face and replaced her spider earrings with golden leaves. Sesame and Tiptoe had put on dresses, while Ping and

Brilliance had wrapped themselves up in their best and brightest outfits. Kelpie looked thunderous in a short bluebell dress which showed her knees. Flea sniffed doubtfully at the dress's curly blue hem and sneezed.

The last dandelion seed spiralled off the dandelion clock. Dame Fuddle and Dame Lacewing both emerged from the Butterfly Stables with their butterflies, Zest and Fraction.

"Off we go!" said Dame Fuddle in excitement, hitching up her bright yellow daffodil gown and climbing on

to Zest, her rather fat Orange Tip butterfly. "Head for the Wood Stump!"

Dame Lacewing silently mounted Fraction as the Naughty Fairies scrambled on to Pong, Ping's enormous emperor dragonfly. They took off in a ragged line, soaring up and over the Hedge and down again into the

Meadow on the other side.

The Wood Stump lay in the middle of the Meadow. Its hollow inside was large enough to hold more than a thousand fairies. It was used as a place for meetings, banquets, competitions and the Moonlit Market, which took place once a month when the moon was full.

A bored looking pixie was standing at the entrance to the Wood Stump as the Naughty Fairies, Dame Fuddle and Dame Lacewing tethered Pong and the butterflies outside.

"Names," said the pixie.

"Dame Fuddle of St Juniper's!" said Dame Fuddle, hauling up a strap on her daffodil dress. "Dame Lacewing of the same! Brilliance, Nettle, Kelpie, Tiptoe, Sesame and Ping, representatives of the student body!"

Kelpie clung tightly to Flea with one hand and tugged at the hem of her bluebell dress with the other. "I'm sure

everyone can see my pants," she muttered at Ping as the Naughty Fairies followed Dame Fuddle and Dame Lacewing through the vast archway of the Wood Stump's central hall.

"It is a bit short," Ping admitted. "Just don't move too fast, and you'll be OK."

The hall was already full of magical creatures. Fairies, elves, goblins, gnomes and pixies stood around

chatting, squabbling, shouting and laughing. In the very centre of the hall stood a vast, circular mushroom table. Smaller mushroom stools were placed around it, with a magnificent multicoloured fungi throne at one end. All around the mushroom sat the most important members of the Bluebell Ball Committee.

"Here is where you and your friends

will be sitting, Brilliance!" said Dame Fuddle brightly, coming to a halt beside a table on the edge of the hall. "Dame Lacewing and I are at the High Mushroom! Remember to vote whenever we do!"

"And try to behave," said Dame Lacewing in a defeated voice.

The Naughty Fairies settled down at their table.

"Why isn't anyone sitting on the fungi throne?" asked Tiptoe, peering up at the High Mushroom.

"That's for the Lady Nymph," said Nettle.

The Naughty Fairies gasped.

"The *Lady Nymph* comes to the Bluebell Ball?" asked Sesame in amazement. "But she's so important!"

"So's the Ball," said Nettle. "The Fairy King and Queen come to it, you know."

"But the Lady Nymph is the *Keeper of*

the Wood!" said Tiptoe in awe.

"I heard that the trees get out of the Lady Nymph's way when she goes for a walk," said Kelpie.

"Even important people like the Lady Nymph must enjoy a good party," said Brilliance.

"The Lady Nymph's much bigger than us," said Ping. "She'll never fit on that tiddly fungi throne."

"She won't really come to the meeting or the Ball," said Brilliance. "The throne is just shambolic."

"Symbolic," Nettle corrected.

"Whatever," Brilliance said. "It means that the Lady Nymph is here in *spirit*."

"What are we voting for, by the way?" asked Sesame, looking around.

"If you're voting for Best Dressed Fairy," drawled a voice, "then St Juniper's is totally at the bottom of the pile."

Smirking at the Naughty Fairies from

a nearby table was a group of fairies dressed in pink rose-petal dresses.

"Ambrosia Academy," Nettle groaned. "That's all we need."

Ambrosia Academy was St Juniper's most bitter rival. With its gleaming toadstool turrets, perfect flutterball pitch and sparkling moat of morning dew, it was everything a fairy school was supposed to be – and everything that St Juniper's was not.

"I mean," went on the pink-clad fairy who had spoken, "what does your Head Teacher think she looks like in that awful old daffodil? Daffs are so common."

The rest of the Ambrosia Academy table sniggered.

Kelpie jumped up.

"Kelpie?" said Ping. "Your—"

"Later," said Kelpie. She marched across to the Ambrosia Academy table. "Watch it, Glitter," she snarled at the fairy who had spoken.

The Ambrosia fairies burst out laughing.

"Nice bumblewool pants, Kelpie!" crowed Glitter. "Oooh, itchy!"

"I tried to tell you your pants were showing," Ping protested as Kelpie turned red and hurried back to the Naughty Fairies' table, tugging hard at her dress hem.

"Dame Fuddle just put up her hand," said Sesame urgently.

The Naughty Fairies flung their hands in the air.

"What did we just vote for?" asked Tiptoe.

Brilliance frowned at the High Mushroom. "Nothing," she said eventually. "Dame Fuddle was just scratching her nose."

At last, the voting began. Copying Dame Fuddle and Dame Lacewing, the Naughty Fairies voted for the menu

(wild garlic leaves stuffed with raspberries, sparkling elderberry juice, bird cherry and blackthorn puddings); the theme (Woodland Wonderland); and the dress code (Dewdrops and Moondust). The meeting droned on. Fireflies emerged from knotholes in the Wood Stump and sparked up their tails as the daylight darkened to evening.

When a snooty-looking elf called for a vote on a band called the Rinker Tinkerbells, the Naughty Fairies voted once again.

The elf counted the votes. "The vote is carried," he said in a deep voice. "This Committee will engage the Rinker Tinkerbells as the band for the evening. The next point on the agenda is . . ."

"Trust St Juniper's to vote for the Stinker Tinkerbells," said Glitter in a loud voice.

"I'll thump Glitter the next time she says something stupid," said Kelpie through gritted teeth.

"This Ball is going to be the worst

ever," said Glitter, even louder.

Kelpie stayed where she was.

"Why aren't you thumping her, Kelpie?" asked Brilliance.

"She'll laugh at my pants again," muttered Kelpie.

"Leave it to me," said Ping.

Casually, Ping dug her hand into her pocket and pulled out something which looked like a tiny green frog. Pretending to stretch, she flung the little frog over her head. It landed neatly in Glitter's lap – and exploded

with a very loud and very smelly bang.

"Urgh!" squealed Glitter, jumping to her feet.

Several nearby tables turned and looked suspiciously at the Ambrosia Academy fairies. Four nearby pixies pinched their noses and muttered to each other in disgust.

The Naughty Fairies roared with laughter.

"Brilliant!" said Brilliance.

"That was a fart frog, wasn't it?" said Nettle, grinning at Ping. "I read about those in *Mischief Monthly*."

"That wasn't just any old fart frog," said Ping. "That was a trump toad. Trump toads are much, *much* smellier."

Glitter stormed over to the Naughty Fairies' table.

"*You,*" she spluttered at Ping.

"Did you hear something?" Ping asked the others in a puzzled voice.

"No," said Nettle.

"Not a word," said Brilliance.

Kelpie waved her hand in front of her face. "There's a bit of a stink, though," she said.

Sesame and Tiptoe giggled.

Glitter leaned across the table towards Ping. "You want a fight?" she hissed. "I'll give you a fight. No one makes a fool out of me and gets away with it. I challenge you – *to the Bramble Run*!"

3

The Bramble Run

The Naughty Fairies gasped.

"The Bramble Run is forbidden by fairy law," said Nettle uneasily.

"Since when did the ragbag fairies of St Juniper's care about laws?" Glitter spat in fury.

"It's forbidden for a reason," Sesame began, with a worried expression on her face. "It's the most dangerous—"

"Do you accept the challenge, Ping?" demanded Glitter.

"Of course," said Ping in a breezy voice. "The Bramble Run doesn't scare me."

"Tomorrow at sunrise," Glitter said with a fierce nod. "At the Bramble Patch. If you're not there, then everyone will know that you're a *coward*."

"I can't believe you just agreed to the Bramble Run, Ping," said Sesame in an awestruck voice as Glitter marched back to her table. "Aren't you scared?"

Ping shook her head.

"You do know what the Bramble Run is, don't you, Ping?" Kelpie checked.

Ping thought. "No," she said. "What is it?"

"It's the most terrifying fairy challenge in the world," Brilliance said.

"You have to race Glitter through the middle of the Bramble Patch in the Meadow," said Tiptoe.

"There's about a hundred twists and turns," added Nettle.

"There are thorns as sharp as Flea's stinger all the way along, ready to slice you into pieces," said Kelpie.

Flea sneezed and waggled his stinger enthusiastically.

Ping shrugged. "I can fly rings

around Glitter, thorns or no thorns."

"Sure you can," said Brilliance. "When you can see where you're going."

"What do you mean?" Ping asked.

"You have to wear a blindfold," said Nettle gently.

Ping stared at her friends. "Ah," she said.

"Bramble Run!" chanted the Ambrosia Academy fairies. "Bramble Run! Bramble Run!"

"Silence in the corner there!" shouted an extremely tall blue-haired fairy sitting at the High Mushroom. "This is a committee meeting, not a raucous flutterball match!"

The Ambrosia fairies went quiet and smiled daintily at the blue-haired fairy. All the gnomes, goblins, pixies and fairies in the room turned and stared at the Naughty Fairies. Dame Lacewing rose to her feet with a scary expression on her face.

"It wasn't us!" Brilliance said indignantly. "Honest, Dame Lacewing!"

"We've been really good!" Tiptoe protested.

"In future, Dame Fuddle," said the blue-haired fairy in an extremely chilly voice, "please choose your committee members more carefully."

Dame Fuddle blushed. Looking pale with anger, Dame Lacewing sat down again very slowly.

"Typical," said Kelpie.

Another half a dandelion drifted past. One or two fireflies fell asleep, and had to be poked awake. At long last, the final decisions were made, and the meeting came to an end.

"There wasn't even any food," said Tiptoe sulkily, as the Naughty Fairies stretched their aching wings and stood up from the table.

Dame Lacewing marched over to the Naughty Fairies' table. "Not a word," she warned, as Brilliance opened her mouth.

"I'm never going to be good again," said Nettle as they followed Dame Lacewing and Dame Fuddle outside to Pong and the butterflies. "It's just not worth it."

"Tomorrow," Glitter hissed, barging

into Ping on the way out. "Sunrise. And may the best fairy win!"

"Dame Lacewing wouldn't even *listen* to what we told her about Ambrosia Academy," said Brilliance furiously as the Naughty Fairies sat in their dormitory that evening. "Even when we've done nothing wrong, we still get detentions."

"Stuff the detentions," said Ping. "What about the Bramble Run?"

The Bramble Run was a problem.

"I suppose you have to do it?" asked Sesame at last.

"Of course I do," said Ping. "But how?"

"Practise," suggested Tiptoe.

"It's tomorrow," protested Ping. "I haven't got time!"

"Get there early," said Nettle.

"The challenge is at sunrise," said Kelpie. "That *is* early."

"We'll get there *earlier* than early,"

said Brilliance with determination. She stuck out her fist. "Naughty Fairies!"

This was the code for Naughty Fairy mischief.

"Niggly fop," said Nettle, putting her fist on Brilliance's.

"Nude flying," offered Tiptoe.

"No fun," said Ping, adding her fist to the pile.

"Nude flying down the Bramble Run would be no fun at all," said Kelpie wisely. "Nearly four."

"Nasty forns," said Sesame.

Puzzled, the Naughty Fairies looked at Sesame.

"What?" asked Brilliance.

"Forns," insisted Sesame. "On brambles. *You* know."

"Oh, *thorns*," said the rest of the Naughty Fairies together.

"That's what I *said*," said Sesame patiently.

"Fair enough," said Brilliance with a

sigh. "Fly, fly . . ."

" . . . to the SKY!" chorused the others, and flung their hands in the air.

"No sleep tonight," said Brilliance, as everyone put their hands down again.

Tiptoe looked at her comfy foxglove sleeping bag. "None at all?" she said in dismay.

Brilliance shook her head. "We have to go to the Bramble Patch and help Ping to practise the Bramble Run."

"But it will be dark," said Nettle.

"That's the point," said Brilliance. "If Ping can fly the Bramble Run in the dark, she can fly it in a blindfold. Isn't it a brilliant idea?"

"When are we going to sleep?" protested Sesame.

"During tomorrow's detention of course," Brilliance said with a shrug. "Let's go. We haven't got any time to waste."

*

The Bramble Run stretched through the middle of the enormous Bramble Patch in the Meadow. There were thorny branches above, below and on both sides of any fairy unwise enough to try and fly it.

The Run was almost impossible in the dark. Ping practised it slowly at first, with the other Naughty Fairies shouting encouragement in the moonlit Meadow.

"Left a bit, Ping!"

"Watch out for that blackberry . . ."

"There's a spider web just above you, Ping – slowly now . . ."

"There's a HUGE thorn about two millisquirts from your bum, Ping . . ."

Ping practised and practised until her wings ached. Slowly, a pale light began to filter through the bramble leaves. *Thorn*, Ping thought to herself as she wearily traced the route again. *Thorn,*

thorn, web web, thorn, berry, web, branch . . .

"Glitter will be here at any moment," said Brilliance, checking the horizon. "How are you feeling, Ping?"

"Like I've been run down by a hedgehog," muttered Ping.

"You won't go too fast, will you?" said Tiptoe anxiously.

"Please be careful," begged Sesame.

The sun peeped above the horizon. There was a whirr of dainty wings, and three Ambrosia Academy fairies arrived on a nearby bramble leaf.

"Oh," said Glitter, staring at Ping. "You're here."

"You thought she wouldn't show up," Brilliance challenged. "Well, she did. So now you have to do the Bramble Run as well."

Glitter looked worried. She went into a huddle with her two friends.

"Glitter hasn't practised," said

Sesame. "Her wings are shaking, look!"

"Let's go," said Ping, bouncing up and down and trying to sound energetic.

"The blindfolds, Gloss," Glitter said at last, holding out her hand.

The taller of the two other fairies silently passed a pair of woven moss scarves to Glitter. Glitter tied one around her eyes, and Ping took the other.

"Everyone knows the rules," said

Brilliance. "The first fairy to come out the other side of the Bramble Run is the winner."

Glitter and Ping nodded.

"Good luck," said Brilliance. "On your wings. Get set. *Go!*"

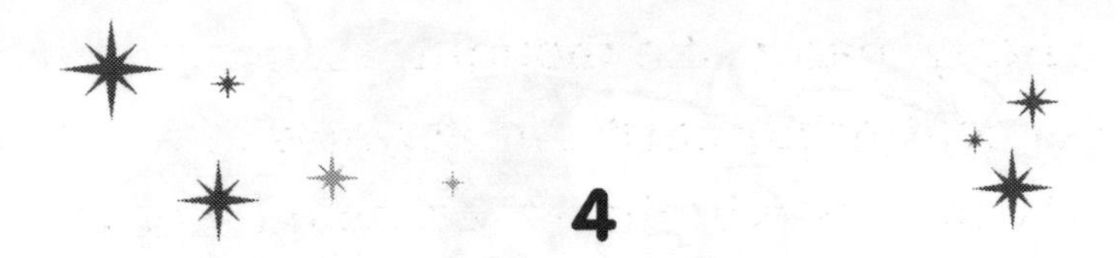

4
Disaster!

Ping felt the whoosh of Glitter's wings as the Ambrosia Academy fairy raced into the mouth of the Bramble Run. She followed as quickly as she dared.

Thorn, she thought to herself. The mossy scarf felt soft and warm on her face as she flew through the brambles. *Thorn, thorn, web web . . .* "Ow!"

A thorn had scraped across her arm. Her heart hammering, Ping veered a little further to the left. *Thorn,* she thought desperately. *Berry, web? Or was it web, berry?*

Dimly she heard the others shouting encouragement. The mouth of the Run wasn't far off now – Ping could feel it.

Berry, berry, she thought, concentrating hard. *Not far now . . .*

"Glitter is winning!" screamed Nettle. "Come on, Ping!"

Ping put on a reckless burst of speed. There was a stabbing sensation, and a horrible tearing sound – and Ping felt herself falling.

"She's waking up."

"Tickle her nose, Kelpie."

"How's that going to help, Sesame? It'll just make her sneeze."

"Stop quarrelling, you two! Kelpie, go and get some rainwater. Maybe we could splash her awake."

Ping opened her eyes. Her five friends rushed to her side.

"Are you OK?" Tiptoe quavered.

Ping stared up at the unfamiliar flowerpot ceiling over her head. "Where am I?" she asked groggily.

"In my study," came Dame

Lacewing's voice. "And in a great deal of trouble."

Ping groaned. She shut her eyes again and tried to roll over, but her wings felt wrong and she couldn't do it. "What have I done to myself?" she whispered.

"You've torn both your wings to pieces, you silly little fairy," said Dame Lacewing, briskly pressing a piece of damp moss to Ping's forehead. "I have performed a temporary healing spell. You must stay completely still for the next three days. Whatever happens, *do not move your wings*. If you try and fly too soon, the healing spell will break. Nature help you if that happens."

Ping gulped.

Dame Lacewing tucked in Ping's grass-weave blanket with some force. "I've seen some stupid things in my time at St Juniper's," she said, "but attempting the Bramble Run has to be the stupidest."

"Will we get detentions, Dame Lacewing?" asked Sesame unhappily.

"Worse," said Dame Lacewing. "You will all have to live with the blame if Ping never flies again."

A tear plopped off Tiptoe's nose.

"You must stay here, Ping," said Dame Lacewing in a slightly gentler voice. "No school for you until next week. Pipsqueak will keep you company. Dame Taffeta is expecting the rest of you for Science."

"But we haven't had breakfast yet," Tiptoe began.

"Breakfast is the least of your worries," said Dame Lacewing grimly. "Now, out."

"Glitter cheated, by the way," Brilliance whispered on the way past the mossy couch where Ping was lying. "Her blindfold had two little eyeholes cut into it. Silly, scheming—"

"Out!" roared Dame Lacewing.

And the Naughty Fairies scuttled away, leaving Ping alone.

If she craned her neck, Ping could see out of Dame Lacewing's study window to the dandelion clock in the courtyard. She'd never known the seeds to drop off the clock so slowly. No lessons for the rest of the week had sounded fantastic – but lying around all day was going to be the most boring thing in the world. Her wings ached, and she felt sore from head to toe.

She spent some of the morning thinking about revenge. But before long, more unwelcome things crowded into her head. *I'll never fly again*, she thought morosely. *I'll have to stay on the ground for ever. I'll be no better than a pixie.*

Ping was about to die of boredom

when a shiny brown head appeared at the window of Dame Lacewing's study. Pipsqueak honked nervously and hid underneath Dame Lacewing's desk.

"Boing!" said Ping. She'd never been so pleased to see a flea in her life. "You came back!"

Boing winked at her and sniffed at

Dame Lacewing's window sill.

And Ping had the most fantastic idea.

There were only three days left until the Bluebell Ball. As the weather was fine, Ping had been resting outside in the sunny Sports Field, and her friends had joined her whenever they could. Lessons grew more and more riotous as fairies ignored their teachers and discussed their outfits. Dame Fuddle's Fairy Deportment class was suddenly the most popular class of the week, with all the older fairies paying close attention to Dame Fuddle's curtseying instructions and dancing tips.

Even the Naughty Fairies were at last interested in the Ball.

"I'm making my dress out of a piece of honeysuckle I've seen at the top of the ivy-covered fence," Brilliance announced on the morning of the Ball. It was break time, and the Naughty

Fairies were sitting in the Sports Field with Ping. "It's cream and pink and gold – all my favourite colours. I'll pick it this afternoon so it's really fresh for tonight."

"I'm wearing red rose-petal trousers," said Nettle. "There's no law against trousers for the Bluebell Ball, is there?"

Sesame was going to use a primrose, and Tiptoe had her eye on some pale pink campion she'd seen by the Hedge.

"I'm not dressing up," said Kelpie, cuddling Flea.

"Not even a bit?" Sesame checked.

"Maybe some extra bumblewool around the hem of my dress," Kelpie said after a moment. "To make it longer."

"What are you going to wear, Ping?" Brilliance asked.

Ping gave a start. "What?"

"You haven't heard a word, have you?" demanded Nettle.

"Sorry," said Ping. "I was thinking about . . . something else."

"What?" Brilliance asked.

Ping smirked. "You'll see," she said.

And she refused to say another word.

Traditionally, the Bluebell Ball began at moonrise. Afternoon lessons were cancelled as fairies ran around in panic and excitement, making last-minute changes to their outfits. Those fairies who weren't old enough to attend the Ball were allowed to watch the preparations from their dormitory windows.

"Lord Gallivant!" called Dame Fuddle, trying to pin her rather crumpled starflower tiara in place as she hurried through groups of excited ball-going fairies in the darkening courtyard. "Where is our night transport? We are going to be late!"

Lord Gallivant the butterfly-riding

teacher pushed his mouse-fur ball cloak casually over one shoulder, so that its bright marigold lining could be seen. He opened the doors to the Butterfly Stables with a flourish. The fairies cheered when they saw a row of elegant hawkmoths snorting and tossing their furry heads.

"I have spent several weeks catching and training them for tonight," Lord Gallivant added proudly.

"You are marvellous, Gracious!" simpered Dame Taffeta, fastening the neck of her cornflower cape. "And I love your cloak!"

"What, this old thing?" said Lord Gallivant casually, tweaking his cloak once again. A flash of bright red pimpernel breeches clashed horribly with the marigold cloak lining.

"I saw Lord Gallivant stitching that cloak in the Butterfly Stables last

night," Sesame whispered to the others. "He's more excited about his outfit than anyone else."

"Each moth will carry two fairies," said Dame Lacewing, adjusting her own purple nightshade hood. "Please wait until I call your names, and then take your moth."

"I want the furriest one," said Kelpie as the fairies shuffled forward, tripping over their gowns and trying not to dirty their new petal shoes. "It will remind me of Flea."

"It was really unfair of Dame Lacewing to make you leave Flea in the dormitory," said Brilliance.

"He doesn't like the dark much," said Kelpie gloomily. "And his cold is still quite bad. It's probably for the best."

Nettle glanced over her shoulder. "What are you doing back there, Ping?" she asked.

Ping emerged from a shadowy corner

of the courtyard. "Me?" she said. "Oh, nothing."

"Tiptoe and Ping," called Dame Lacewing. "Take that moth in the corner there. You know the way to the Bluebell Glade, don't you? It's on the far edge of the Wood beside the Stream. Follow the others and you can't go wrong." Dame Lacewing paused. "Well," she said in a weary voice, "*you* probably could. But please – don't."

"Go without me, Tiptoe," Ping whispered, as Tiptoe took hold of the moth's reins.

"Aren't you coming?" Tiptoe gasped.

"Oh I'll be there," said Ping. "I've just arranged . . . alternative transport. Save me a place, will you? I might be a little late." And she disappeared into the gloom again.

"Everyone ready?" called Dame Fuddle, before the Naughty Fairies could chase after Ping and ask her what she was planning. "The Ball awaits!"

And in a flurry of moth wings and multicoloured petals, the fairies took off into the night.

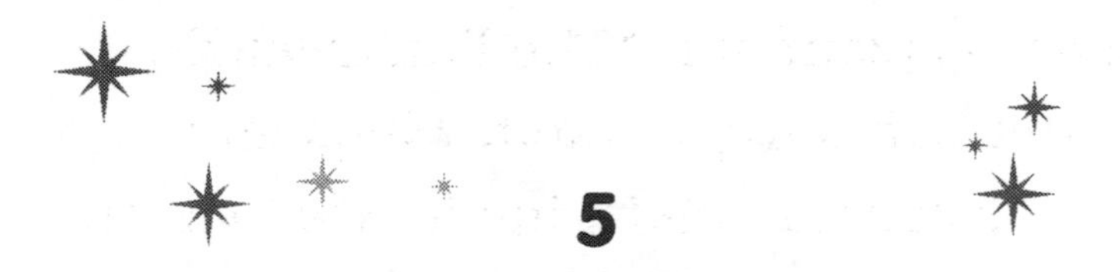

5
The Bluebell Ball

The Bluebell Glade looked wonderful in the cool glow of the moon. The ground was a sea of blue, dotted with soft green moss and the bright flash of fairies in their finest gowns. Beneath the stately bluebell columns, hundreds of tables were laid with white petal cloths, crystal glasses and shell plates. Pixies in smart bluebell coats with lily-petal napkins draped over their arms were whisking around with pitchers of sparkling elderberry juice. Fireflies danced overhead in clouds, adding their brightness to the occasion.

"Look at the cake!" Tiptoe squealed.

A towering cake of blackberries,

clover honey, cream and sugared violets stood on a polished crystal table in the middle of the Glade.

"Trust you to spot the food," said Nettle with a sigh.

"When are the King and Queen coming?" asked Sesame in high excitement.

Thousands of bluebells began to ring high notes, low notes and in-between notes, all in tune with each other. Everyone turned to see the white-haired Fairy King in a midnight blue cloak and a crystal crown step into the Glade. By his side was the Queen, her wings shimmering like stardust and her dress as bright as a moonbeam.

Soon, the guests settled down at their tables for dinner. The Naughty Fairies spotted the Ambrosia Academy fairies being shown to a nearby table by a bluebell-coated pixie, and stuck out their tongues at Glitter.

"What a horrible dress Glitter's wearing," said Brilliance in satisfaction. "She looks like a fat, frilly snowflake."

The others giggled.

"There's Ping!" said Kelpie, sitting down on a shiny brown pebble stool and taking a slurp of elderberry fizz. "Where's she been?"

"Somehow, I think we're about to find out," said Nettle.

"She's talking to the pixie who showed Glitter to her table," said Sesame with interest. "She's giving him something – look."

They watched with curiosity as the pixie waiter pocketed whatever Ping had given him and walked away quickly. Ping strolled over to the Naughty Fairies' table and settled down on an empty pebble stool.

"What have you done?" asked Tiptoe in an eager voice.

Ping nodded at Glitter and the

Ambrosia Academy table. "There's something a bit odd about Glitter's stool," she said. "Don't you think?"

The Naughty Fairies stared at the shiny brown pebble Glitter was sitting on. One end of the pebble opened a beady black eye and winked at them.

"That's not a pebble," said Brilliance in astonishment. "It's a flea."

"It's *Boing*!" Sesame gasped.

"I gave that pixie waiter a little something for making sure Glitter sat there," said Ping with a wicked grin.

"I was right the other day, about training fleas. You can train a clever flea like Boing to do anything you want. You just need time. And I've had plenty of that this week. Now, just sit back and enjoy the show."

Ping pursed her lips and made a quick, chirruping noise to get Boing's attention. The flea blinked at her as she stretched out her arm and casually clicked her fingers. And Glitter got the fright of her life as her stool rose into the air at an alarming speed, carrying her with it.

Boing soared upwards, over the crystal tables and the shell plates, over the pixie waiters and even over the Fairy King and Queen, with Glitter wailing and clinging on to his back. Everyone in the Bluebell Glade gasped and stared in horror.

"Oh no!" Tiptoe squealed. "Boing is heading straight for the—"

SPLAT

"Cake," Ping finished cheerfully.

Boing had landed feet first in the magnificent berry-topped confection. Cream and blackberries flew in all directions. Honey exploded from the sides of the cake, and sugared violets fell down on the ball guests like purple rain. Boing shook Glitter off his back, winked at Ping and soared out of the Glade, disappearing into the gloom of the Wood.

A terrible silence fell on the Bluebell Glade as the Fairy King wiped a blob of cream rather frostily from his face. He stared at Glitter, still sprawled in the middle of the cake.

"Who," said the King in a terrifying voice, "Are You?"

"It's m . . . me, Uncle," squeaked Glitter. "G . . . G . . . Glitter."

"Glitter," said the King, in the kind of voice usually saved for slugs. "Remove yourself from that cake. I shall be

speaking to your mother about this."

Glitter burst into tears and rushed out of the Glade, scattering cream and cake crumbs over the guests. Glitter's friends raced after her, toppling over the crystal tables as they went, knocking glasses full of elderberry fizz to the ground and soaking the petal shoes of the shrieking ball guests. The Rinker Tinkerbells did their best to strike up a waltz, but their instruments were covered in blackberries and made a dismal noise. The pixie waiters threw down their lily-petal napkins and tore off their bluebell coats. The tall blue-haired fairy who had taken the final Committee Meeting fainted into Lord Gallivant's arms, and several bluebell flowers dropped from their stems and crashed to the ground, missing the guests by a whisker.

Amid the chaos, the Naughty Fairies stared at Ping in silent wonder.

"That'll teach Glitter not to cheat,"

said Ping in a contented voice.

"PIIIINNNNGGG!" bellowed Dame Lacewing.

The Naughty Fairies leaped out of their skins. The Deputy Head of St Juniper's was bearing down on their table with a face like a boiled carrot.

"How did Dame Lacewing know—" Kelpie began.

"Dame Lacewing always knows," Nettle said.

"Dame Lacewing looks like an angry mosquito," said Sesame.

Tiptoe gave an extremely nervous giggle as Dame Lacewing arrived at the Naughty Fairies' table.

"It wasn't us, Dame Lacewing," began Brilliance hopefully.

"Of course it was you," Dame Lacewing shouted. "I recognised the flea. It will be a miracle if St Juniper's reputation ever recovers from this . . . this *fiasco*. Everyone is leaving. The

Ball is over. *You* have ruined the greatest social event in the fairy calendar!"

The Naughty Fairies stared around at the upended tables and the broken plates, the furious waiters and the crumby, creamy, juicy puddle that had been the cake. It was true. The Fairy King and Queen had vanished, the Rinker Tinkerbells had packed away their instruments and the muttering ball guests were putting on their cloaks and leaving the Glade.

"Whoops," said Ping.

Dame Lacewing took a deep breath. "Now," she said, "you will all stay behind to clear up this mess."

The Naughty Fairies all began talking at once.

"It was Glitter who covered the Fairy King with cream, Dame Lacewing . . ."

"Glitter started it at the Committee Meeting . . ."

". . . She's the one who challenged Ping to the Bramble Run and cheated . . ."

"Don't interrupt me," Dame Lacewing roared. "I want this Glade spotless by sunrise. I don't care if it takes all night."

Ping opened her eyes very wide. "Dame Lacewing," she began.

"We will discuss you in the morning, Ping," said Dame Lacewing in her most deadly voice.

And with a furious swirl of her nightshade cloak, the Deputy Head of St Juniper's marched away through the middle of the mess.

"I didn't like the way Dame Lacewing said 'discuss'," said Ping at last.

Broken bluebells lay sadly among the ruined petal tablecloths and tattered ball slippers as midnight whispered through the Glade. Exhausted, the Naughty Fairies washed the last remaining shell plates and wiped the

last few crystal tables, storing them all neatly in a hole at the base of a nearby beech tree. Dame Lacewing prowled up and down the Glade, her wand jutting out of her belt in a scary sort of way.

"I can't wait to get back to school," said Nettle sleepily, sweeping the mossy ground. "I want to go to bed."

"Don't think we'll be getting much sleep," Tiptoe yawned. "Dame Lacewing wants us in her study before breakfast."

"What if Dame Lacewing makes us apologise to the Fairy King?" said Sesame anxiously.

"What if Dame Lacewing makes us apologise to *Glitter*?" said Brilliance.

"No *way*," said Ping and Kelpie at the same time.

"If I tell you to apologise, you will apologise," said Dame Lacewing, looming up behind the Naughty Fairies and making them jump. "But we will save that for another day."

The teacher narrowed her eyes and stared around. Although the Naughty Fairies hadn't been able to mend the broken bluebells, the rest of the Glade looked immaculate.

"That will do," said Dame Lacewing at last.

The Naughty Fairies breathed a sigh of relief, and went to find their moths. It was time to go back to school.

Dame Lacewing and the Naughty Fairies put their heads down and clung on tight as their moths headed back to St Juniper's, zigzagging noiselessly among the dark tree trunks and keeping to the shadows. Strange and dangerous things lived in the Wood at night. Things that the fairies were keen to avoid.

Suddenly an owl swooped down from a treetop, its beak wide. The fairies screamed – their moths veered out of

reach – and the owl's beak met thin air.

"Everyone OK?" said Dame Lacewing sharply as the owl screeched its disappointment and flew back to its tree on silent wings.

"I'm still here," said Nettle, clinging on around Brilliance's waist.

"Me too," squeaked Brilliance.

"Sesame?" Dame Lacewing called. "Kelpie?"

"Here," shouted Sesame.

"Just," grumbled Kelpie. "Owls should be banned."

"Which leaves Tiptoe and Ping," said Dame Lacewing, peering over her shoulder into the gloom.

"Ping's gone!" Tiptoe panted, flying up beside Nettle and Brilliance. "She was right behind me just now, and then she just . . . *fell off*!"

6

The Lady Nymph

Ping opened her eyes. She was lying on her back in a mossy glade she didn't recognise. The moon shone down, a burning white light in the black sky.

Trying to sit up, an awful agony tore through Ping's wings and she squealed with pain. Collapsing back again, Ping groaned as she remembered Dame Lacewing's words.

If you try and fly too soon, the healing spell will break . . . Nature help you if that happens . . . Nature help you . . .

When the owl had swooped, Ping had slid off her moth's back. Automatically, she had stretched out her wings . . . and crashed to the ground.

Ping squeezed her eyes tightly shut. *There's no point feeling sorry for yourself,* she thought fiercely as the tears oozed out through her eyelids.

"Help," she whispered to the moon. "Oh, help. HELP!"

A vast shadow fell across the glade, and a cool hand swept Ping from the ground. Ping went rigid with terror as she stared up into an enormous, pale-skinned face.

"Ouch," said the Lady Nymph, looking at Ping's wings with long-lashed blue eyes. "That must really, *really* hurt."

Ping couldn't speak as the Lady Nymph moved through the glade and into the shadowy trees. She lay as still as she could in the Lady Nymph's palm and stared up at her rescuer. She had the most beautiful face that Ping had ever seen.

"Nearly there," said the Lady Nymph.

Her voice sounds like water, thought Ping sleepily. The steady movement of the Lady Nymph was soothing, and her wings felt better already.

The sound of water grew closer. Ping listened. It wasn't the Lady Nymph's voice any more. It was a spring – a rushing, bubbling sound full of splash and life. Ping felt the cool spray on her forehead as the Lady Nymph laid her down beside the water and placed a soft downy feather under her head.

"This won't take long," said the Lady Nymph gently.

Ping drifted in and out of consciousness. She was vaguely aware of the Lady Nymph moving around her, her gown rustling softly in the grass as she scooped water from the spring. The cool scent of bluebells and the sharp tang of icy moonlight drifted through Ping's senses.

"Drink," said the Lady Nymph.

Ping tipped her head and gulped from the acorn cup that the Lady Nymph was carefully holding between her long, slender fingertips. She spluttered and coughed.

"How do your wings feel now, Ping?" asked the Keeper of the Wood.

Ping moved her wings very cautiously. Then she moved them a little more.

"Better," she said. "Stronger than before." She stood up and flapped her wings. To her delight, she soared off the moss like an arrow.

"Thank you, my Lady," she said shyly, drifting back down to the ground again.

Ping couldn't look at her rescuer as she said this. Somehow she knew that all the naughty things she had ever done would appear in her eyes for the Keeper of the Wood to see.

Ping felt a cool kiss on the top of her head. Then there was a whirl of light

and wind, and Ping was lifted off the ground. She twirled giddily, spinning through clouds and stars and moonlight – and found, to her astonishment, that she had landed safely in the courtyard of St Juniper's.

The dawn was stealing over the tops of the flowerpot towers, casting long shadows at Ping's feet. A dandelion seed spiralled off the dandelion clock. In a daze, Ping picked up the seed and twirled it between her fingers. Had she really seen the Lady Nymph? How had the Keeper of the Wood known her name? She peered over her shoulder at her wings. They seemed bigger than before, and were the same colour as the palest bluebells in the Wood.

A shadow detached itself from the flowerpots and hurried across the courtyard. Ping was grasped by two strong hands. She squeaked in terror.

"Ping!" said Dame Lacewing in a

peculiar voice. "Are you all right? We searched for you when you fell, but couldn't find you! I thought . . ." Dame Lacewing stopped. "Well," she said, "never mind what I thought. You're here now."

Ping peered more closely at Dame Lacewing. "You're not crying, are you Dame Lacewing?" she said.

"Don't be ridiculous," said Dame Lacewing.

"It's just . . ." Ping stopped at the ferocious look in Dame Lacewing's eye.

The teacher gripped her more tightly.

"Um," said Ping. "You're not going to . . . hug me or anything, are you Dame Lacewing?"

Dame Lacewing let go.

"Am I in trouble?" Ping asked, rubbing her arms.

"No more than usual," Dame Lacewing sighed. "Show me your wings. How did you get back here with your injuries?"

Ping fluttered her wings, feeling shy. "I got new wings," she said. "From the Lady Nymph. She rescued me. Honest, Dame Lacewing! I'm telling the truth!"

Dame Lacewing sighed. "For once,"

she said, "I believe you, Ping. Now go and get your friends and meet me in my study. We are going to find the Fairy King and you are going to apologise for making your flea jump into the cake."

Ping stared at her shoes. "Do we have to apologise to Glitter too, Dame Lacewing?" she asked.

"I am sure," said Dame Lacewing, "that Glitter was sitting on your flea purely by chance. Don't you agree?"

Ping opened her mouth. Then she shut it again.

"Yes, Dame Lacewing," she said with a grin.

Also available from
Hodder Children's Books

Tricksy Pixie

The Naughty Fairies face a challenge – to play the best trick on Bindweed the garden pixie. Their prank is SO good that Bindweed quits St Juniper's. Who will look after the school grounds now?

The Naughty Fairies of course!

Also available from
Hodder Children's Books

An Utter Flutter

It's the Flutterball Final, and the Naughty Fairies make an awesome team, But their butterflies go missing – and without them, there's no way they can win. Can the Naughty Fairies find the thieves and get their butterflies back?

Also available from
Hodder Children's Books

Never Hug a Slug

Panic strikes when the Humans decide to tidy up their garden. Could this be the end for St Juniper's? The Naughty Fairies think they have the answer – but it's going to be slimy!

Also available from
Hodder Children's Books

Potion Commotion

Detention is NOT Kelpie's idea of fun on her flutterday. A trip to the beach should make up for it! But when uninvited guests pay a visit, it looks as if Kelpie's flutterday is going to be one BIG disaster.

Also available from
Hodder Children's Books

Spider Insider

Fashion and the Naughty Fairies don't mix. So how will they beat Ambrosia Academy at the Fairy Fashion Show? Some extra-special spider silk is their only hope to stop a fashion fiasco!